• A FRANK ASCH BEAR BOOK •

PANCAKES
IN PAJAMAS

• FRANK ASCH •

ALADDIN
New York   London   Toronto   Sydney   New Delhi

ALADDIN

An imprint of Simon & Schuster Children's Publishing Division

1230 Avenue of the Americas, New York, New York 10020

First Aladdin paperback edition March 2019

Copyright © 2018 by Frank Asch

Also available in an Aladdin hardcover edition.

All rights reserved, including the right of reproduction

in whole or in part in any form.

ALADDIN and related logo are registered trademarks of Simon & Schuster, Inc.

For information about special discounts for bulk purchases,

please contact Simon & Schuster Special Sales at 1-866-506-1949

or business@simonandschuster.com.

The Simon & Schuster Speakers Bureau can bring authors to your live event.

For more information or to book an event contact the

Simon & Schuster Speakers Bureau at 1-866-248-3049

or visit our website at www.simonspeakers.com.

Series designed by Karina Granda

The text of this book was set in Olympian LT Std.

Manufactured in China 1218 SCP

2 4 6 8 10 9 7 5 3 1

Library of Congress Control Number 2017952098

ISBN 978-1-4814-8060-4 (hc)

ISBN 978-1-4814-8061-1 (pbk)

ISBN 978-1-4814-8062-8 (eBook)

To Paci, Ariah, Jaya, and Scott

One Saturday morning at breakfast, Baby
Bear said, "This is so much fun! You know
what I wish? I wish we could stay in our
pajamas and eat pancakes all day long!"

"I think that's a great idea!" said Papa Bear.

"Me too," said Mama Bear.

"What happens now?" asked Baby Bear as he helped clear the table.

"We can do lots of things," said Papa Bear.

"I'd like to go back to bed," said Mama Bear.

"Me too," said Papa Bear.

"And read stories?!" cried Baby Bear.

Back in their big cozy bed, Mama and Papa Bear read tales about timid tigers and fishy goldfish, penguins that couldn't find their suspenders, and polar bears in spaceships looking for a new planet until—*zzzz*—they all fell sound asleep.

Baby Bear was first to open his eyes.
  "Wake up, Mama! Wake up, Papa!"
he cried.

"Gosh, it sure was a busy week," said Papa. "I really needed that nap."

"Me too," said Mama.

"Me three!" said Baby Bear.

After their nap, the Bear family played
board games and threw cards into a hat.

Then they took a long walk in the park.

At the playground, Mama Bear played with Baby Bear on the swings, and Papa Bear played with him on the seesaw.

Then they rode bikes all over town.

"All this fresh air and exercise
make me hungry," said Papa Bear.
   "Me too," said Mama.
   "Me three!" said Baby Bear.
   "Let's stop at Pete's Pancakes for
lunch," said Papa Bear.

"Tell me," asked Pete when he brought them their pancakes, "why are you all wearing your pajamas and riding bikes today? Is it some kind of a holiday?"

"I guess you might say it's Pancakes in Pajamas Day," said Papa Bear.

"That's right," said Mama Bear. "And we're part of the bicycle parade."

"That sounds like fun," said Pete. "If you wait a minute, I'll ask my wife and kids and we'll join you."

As the Bear family rode through town, family after family put on

their pajamas and joined the
Pancakes in Pajamas Day parade.

When the parade reached the town square . . .

. . . everyone enjoyed an incredible,

edible Pancakes in Pajamas party!

On the way home, Baby Bear fell fast asleep in his bicycle seat.

"What a wonderful day we had," said Papa Bear as he carried Baby Bear up to his bed.

"I hope we can do this again sometime soon."

"Me too," said Mama Bear.

"Me three," murmured Baby Bear.